APHRODITE TERRA

STORIES ABOUT VENUS

edited by Ian Sales

Whippleshield Books
www.whippleshieldbooks.com
UK

Published by Whippleshield Books
www.whippleshieldbooks.com

ISBN 978-0-9931417-5-1 (paper)
ISBN 978-0-9931417-6-8 (ebook)

Cover by Kay Sales

INTRODUCTION

Back in 2012, I edited an anthology of hard science fiction and fact called *Rocket Science* for Mutation Press. All of its stories took place within the Solar System, and it occurred to me there was more than enough real estate orbiting our Sun to use as settings, or inspirations, for fiction. And this was especially true given recent space probe missions and the fantastic images they were sending back—of Mars, Mercury, the comet 67P/Churyumov-Gerasimenko, Luna, the asteroid Vesta, and now Pluto...

Of course, there's been plenty of science fiction written in the decades since the genre's beginning set entirely within the Solar System—from Leigh Brackett's tales of lost Martian grandeur to John Varley's Eight Worlds. Nonetheless, the idea of a Grand Tour of anthologies—small anthologies, containing no more than half a dozen stories each—seemed like a worthwhile project.

So in late 2013 I picked Venus as my first port of call, chose a title from its landscape, "Aphrodite Terra", and put out a call for submissions. The plan was to produce the book quickly, and have it available for sale at Loncon3, the Worldcon taking place in London in August 2014.

For a variety of reasons, that never happened. I didn't even attend the convention.

I also had another project on the go—the fourth and final book of my Apollo Quartet series of novellas. Except I had decided the final book would be a novel, not a novella. I'd already spent much of the year researching for it, but I needed to get it written.

And then I sold a space opera trilogy to a small press. Two of the three books had been written several years before, but they needed a bit of tidying up. And that third book would need writing from scratch...

So, what with one thing and another, poor *Aphrodite Terra* slipped further and further down the schedule. Until it reached the point where I realised I had to either get it out, or give up on it...

I chose to do the former.

So here it is: the somewhat delayed *Aphrodite Terra*, an anthology of six stories about, set on, or inspired by, the planet Venus. Some of the stories are hard sf, some are not. Some of them take place on Venus, some do not. But all in some way are *about* the planet Venus.

I wanted a literary feel to my mini-anthology more than I wanted a hard sf feel, so that's what drove my selections from the submissions sent me. I wanted stories that used the language of science fiction, but seemed to be written from a perspective a step back from genre. It's perhaps a distinction visible only to myself, but never mind—at least it has resulted in what I think is a collection of interesting stories—

From Heidi Kneale's tale of homelessness and science to Lorraine Schein's fable about female anarchists, from Deborah Walker's poetic colonisation of the Evening Star to Erin Hartshorn's story of a flight from war (Venus at least, it seems, accepts refugees), and from Rosie Oliver's hard sf to EM Edward's densely-written heartland science fiction. Hopefully, there's something in these six short stories readers will find appealing...

And who knows? Maybe that Grand Tour might take another step some time. For now...

Enjoy.

December 2015

GOLDILOCKS ZONE

Heidi Kneale

Lizzi Garret drew her finger through the dust of the fruit bowl. Empty again, like her stomach. In the staff room the scent of coffee and early-morning murmured conversation competed with the rumblings of her stomach.

No fruit. That left milk. Plain, boring, cloying milk. Milk, with no cocoa, no coffee, no sugar. They made her too jittery. With the exception of an apple two days ago and a purloined cookie yesterday, Lizzi's diet during the week had consisted of nothing but the milk from the staff fridge.

At least her rent would be paid this fortnight. Just. As she tipped the frothy white liquid into her mug, her eyes filled with tears. Salt for her milk, and bitter gall for her days. How much longer could she survive?

Had the rent control laws saved her, or merely prolonged the inevitable? With her lease renewal the rent of her tiny studio apartment had gone up ten percent, consuming the money she would have spent on food.

Might as well get it over with. Tilting her head back, Lizzi gulped down the milk, forcing it into her system. At least a human could live on milk alone, somewhat. There was always milk for coffee in the fridge. But couldn't they fill the fruit bowl more often?

She shuddered. Another three hours until gnawing desperation forced her back here to drink more than her fair share. As the morning lab shift arrived, their mouths full of gossip and breakfast, Lizzi beat her retreat.

Work awaited her.

♀

Mars had been colonised—easily so, once the terraformers had jump-started its frozen core back into geothermal activity. This resurrected its magnetic field, which powered the Van Allen Belts, which protected the surface of Mars from solar radiation, et cetera, et cetera. Lizzi didn't care much for geophysics.

Her love lay in the microorganisms that made an atmosphere possible on Mars. Mars had so little atmosphere and Venus so much, so some bright spark figured out a way of harvesting the carbon dioxide-rich air from Venus for the benefit of Mars.

What Lizzi and her team had done was bio-engineer microorganisms to metabolise carbon dioxide into useful oxygen and fixed carbon.

Now that was work worth boasting about! While plants did this sort of thing on Earth all the time, Lizzi's microorganisms were special. They could withstand all kinds of weather extremes, from the thin air on Mars, to the moist confines of a spaceship's CO_2 scrubbers. They could even withstand exposure to the vacuum of space and still wake up when they returned to ideal conditions. Versatile little things. Lizzi loved them so.

Then someone came up with the idea that if the microorganisms could make Venusian air suitable for Mars, why didn't they simply start terraforming Venus? Surely all they had to do was drop the microorganisms into the atmosphere and wait.

Only a politician would say something as stupid as that.

Venus was a harsh world, its Greenhouse Effect run amuck. Lizzi's microorganisms might be hardy, but the only conditions they couldn't bear was the extreme heat and pressure of Venus. Lizzi didn't see how they could engineer them to withstand such a terrible environment. It made her cry. Then again, most things made her cry of late.

The morning milk did not sit well in her stomach. She'd

have terrible wind later. As she walked down the corridor of the research facility, she dashed at her tears with the corner of her lab coat. What she wouldn't give for a slice of bread right now.

Lizzi shared her lab with the other researchers on her team. They worked in shifts around the clock. John Ramey and Elion Fossey would be finishing up by now. In about an hour, Alice Evans would show up, after she'd taken her son to school.

That would give Lizzi enough time to have a good cry.

Lizzi waved her ID pass at the security lock on the door. It beeped, granting her entrance. Her hand closed on the handle, its smoothness comforting. The lab was her true home, not that dingy little studio apartment for which she overpaid.

Here was clean. Here was safe. Here, they paid her, though not enough. Never enough. And there was always milk in the fridge.

She opened the lab door.

"Wait!" cried a voice from inside. A hand raised to forbid her entrance, or possibly to block her view. Elion Fossey, a shirt clasped over his groin, his naked chest starkly white in the artificial light. Clothes draped over lab chairs.

Lizzi squeaked and slammed the door closed. What was that? Her heart tattooed in her chest. She leaned against the door, hoping it would not open. What had she seen? Her cheeks burned.

"Sorry, Lizzi!" Elion shouted through the door. "Just a minute!"

She drew a few more breaths. What was he doing naked in the lab?

From the other side of the door, Elion apologised once more. The handle turned and the door nudged against her back. "Lizzi?"

She gave him room.

A dressed Elion stuck his head out. "I'm so sorry about that. I wasn't expecting you so early."

Lizzi wrapped her arms about her and looked away. She'd come early to work, as hunger had denied her sleep.

He opened the door wider and waited.

Beyond him, a duffel bag sat on the bench next to the computers. Clothes still draped the chairs, but at least Elion had pulled on trousers and an unbuttoned shirt.

Lizzi didn't know where to look. Most improper, for he was married. "What were you doing?" She pressed a fist to her mouth in case anything else should slip out.

He had been alone in the lab. Naked, but alone. He stepped aside, still holding open the door. She did not enter.

"Please don't tell anyone," he begged.

She repeated her question. Who gets naked in a lab?

The voice of fellow researchers echoed down the corridor. "Quick," he urged. "Inside."

Grasping her wrist, he pulled her in. Lizzi squeaked.

He closed the door and listened. The researchers passed by.

Lizzi looked at the duffel bag, open. More clothes lay inside, what looked like folded oxford shirts. For the third time, she asked, "What were you doing?"

"Changing." Elion remained by the door, sheepish.

Lizzi folded her arms tightly across her chest. "Changing?" In the lab? "What's wrong with the locker room?" Every employee got their own locker, for the storing of purses, winter coats, anything they did not wish to bring into the lab. Also, there were showers and a modest laundry facility. Biochemical work could get very smelly.

Elion swallowed. "I didn't want Mark from HR catching me again."

"Catch you doing what?" Lizzi shuffled her feet. Elion stood between her and the door. No escape. She looked to the duffel bag. "Are those... *women's* clothes in there?"

Elion blinked at her. "What?"

Lizzi turned her face away.

A chuckle escaped his lips. "Oh. No, no. Regular clothes."

He left the door and gathered his scattered clothing from about the lab. He was barefoot, his shoes tucked under the desk. From the duffel bag he pulled a pair of socks, but everything else, he shoved in carelessly. "Just ordinary clothes, I'm afraid."

Lizzi inched her way to the door. Elion sat on the chair and pulled on his socks and shoes. He buttoned his shirt and tucked it in, then covered it all with his lab coat.

Lizzi had almost made it to freedom when Elion looked up at her. "We've worked together for nearly a year. Can..." he licked his lips. "Can you keep a secret?"

Her throat constricted. "I don't know. Will it get me fired?"

Elion's mouth opened, then closed. "You? No. Me..." He inhaled some courage. "Please don't tell Mark from HR. Please don't tell anyone."

The door lay behind her now. She snuck a hand to its surface. Could she escape before he stopped her?

He held out his hands to placate her. "I've done nothing wrong." He sank into his chair. From his desk drawer he pulled a sandwich, wrapped in paper. The logo on the wrapper identified the sandwich as having come from the downstairs deli. Lizzi loved that deli, when she could afford to eat there.

That was four months ago. Her mouth watered. What kind of sandwich was it? She stepped forward once, twice.

But Elion didn't open the sandwich. He merely traced the edge of the paper. "John knows, but nobody else. Nobody else can know."

She inhaled. Nothing but lab smell. Was it a chicken sandwich? Ham?

"Lizzi, promise me you won't tell anyone."

She tore her gaze from the sandwich. He was changing

in the lab, because he didn't want to change in the locker room, because Mark from HR would catch Elion again. Catch him at what?

Elion had joined their bioresearch team about a year ago. Sometimes their schedules overlapped. Lizzi liked him—really liked him. He was personable and came up with outside-the-box ideas. But did she really know him?

Now he sat in an office chair, staring at that unopened sandwich before him. His hand hovered over the wrapper.

Open it, Lizzi wanted to say. No, don't. What was worse, an uneaten sandwich, or watching him eat that sandwich in front of her?

His finger snaked under the wrapper and lifted it up. Like opening the petals of a flower, he revealed a beautiful roll with sprouts, cheese and more sticking out the sides. Freed from the confines of paper, the two halves leaned away from each other. Her stomach clenched. How long had it been since she'd embraced such food?

He lifted one half and offered it to her. "Want some?"

Lizzi pounced on the sandwich, nearly snatching away two of Elion's fingers with it. She crammed the sandwich to her face and sank her teeth into the soft, soft bread.

Meat! Glorious meat. And a thick slice of tomato, all sour. A rush of ecstasy flowed in her veins, shutting out the rest of the world. A plethora of flavours blended in her mouth, bringing a rush of saliva. She closed her eyes and bowed her head in gratitude for such wonderful food as she chewed.

Never, never, never had anything ever tasted so good.

When she had swallowed and come back to earth, she opened her eyes.

Elion sat watching her, bemused. A modest bite sat in his half of the sandwich. "Are you all right, Lizzi?"

With awkward embarrassment, Lizzi sank to her office chair. "Thank you for the sandwich."

A smile tugged at the corner of his lips. "Welcome."

Lizzi looked to the sandwich, then up to Elion. "I'll keep your secret."

♀

Of all their Venusian prototypes, Microg 21A variant D had the best chance of survival. The cells could withstand temperatures up to 55 Celsius and pressure up to four atmospheres. Venus had an atmospheric zone that met these criteria. Any bacteria living in that zone could happily munch on carbon dioxide—assuming nothing went wrong.

John Ramey had come up with the genetic coding for 21A-D to grow long silky wisps like a dandelion seed. These wisps enabled it to remain suspended in air.

But 21A-D never remained there for long. Venus suffered storms far beyond anything found on Earth. These storms could easily throw 21A-D up to a higher level of atmosphere, where the dropping temperatures would put it to sleep.

If no storms dispersed 21A-D, it would consume and consume carbon dioxide, breathing out oxygen. Before the cells reached mitosis, they would become too heavy with carbon chains, and drift down into hotter layers to perish.

Why couldn't they get anything just right?

Lizzi studied the sandwich in her hand. The sandwich was just right. It had the best balance of meat and cheese to bread, and not too much lettuce. Some places bulked out their sandwiches with too much lettuce, making it more like a salad than a proper sandwich.

But this...? Her stomach settled down in contentment.

Elion's eyes studied her, but she didn't care. She had a sandwich!

"Am I correct in assuming I'm not the only one with a secret?" Elion took his time eating, more interested in Lizzi than in his own food.

"You first," Lizzi replied. After all, she was not the one caught naked in a lab.

Elion nodded, resigned. "I'm homeless."

Lizzi stopped chewing. "What?" That couldn't be. Elion had a home. She'd been there once for a party. He lived in a small one bedroom unit over by the industrial area. "What happened?"

Elion fiddled with his wedding ring. "When the landlord renewed the lease four months ago, he bumped up the rent. The original tenant couldn't afford it and neither could I." He hung his head. "The tenant had to give up the lease."

Lizzi's chewing slowed. "You were," she hesitated to say it, "subletting?" That was illegal. Rent control laws insisted that only the original tenant could occupy an apartment. But with the rents on new leases skyrocketing over the past ten years, many people were forced out of their homes when their leases expired. "What were you paying?"

"One thousand eight hundred."

"Not bad." Ever since Lizzi's own lease had been put up, she'd been paying one thousand four hundred a week, more than she could truly afford. She'd been putting in bid after bid for any vacancy that came up, only to be shot down. Nobody was willing to rent out even a closet for less than two thousand a week.

For Lizzi, that kind of money was impossible. "So, what happened?"

Elion shrugged. "You know. The usual. I put a bid on a place, some rich DINKs outbid me, and that's that."

Lizzie knew. Advertised rents disappeared a long time ago. When a lease was available, potential renters put in their bid of what they were willing to pay for it. Highest bidder got the lease.

He ran a hand through his hair. "I don't know what I'm going to do. You know Marla, my wife?"

Lizzi nodded. Elion kept a picture of her by his computer. Lizzi had never met her, as Marla lived in another city.

"Her work contract expired three months ago. As she had been planning on moving out here, she didn't reapply. She can get work out here, but until she has a fixed address, nobody'll hire her."

How heartbreaking. Tears welled up in Lizzi's eyes. If Marla had a job, she and Elion would have enough to bid for a lease. But until they could win a lease, she wouldn't have a job.

"So, what have you been doing? Where do you live? How do you survive?" And what about the fixed address required for a job? No wonder he didn't want Mark from HR to know.

Elion shrugged. "I've been living here at the lab, somewhat." He gestured to the duffel bag. "Everything I own is in that."

Clues Lizzi hadn't recognised now came together. She and Elion often worked different shifts, but she always saw him around. How often did she find him snoozing in the staff room after his shift?

She'd even found him asleep in the lab a few times. "Go home," she'd tell him. "Your bed's far more comfortable."

How long had this been going on? Weeks? Months?

Yeah. Four months, or thereabouts. That's when Elion asked to be transferred to the graveyard shift. Night time, even in the city, was no time to be out on the street.

So had he been coming here at the beginning of swing shift, snoozing in odd corners, then working the graveyard, and then catching a morning nap before...? "Where do you go when you leave work?"

He shrugged. "Out and about. I try to spread out my sleep schedule. If I slept here all the time, they'd definitely catch on. Sometimes I go to the movies and sleep in the theatre. Other times I head over to the university. I'll slip into the library, pile a few open books about me, and fall asleep on the table."

The university library trick—that was smooth. How

many times had Lizzi taken a nap at school between classes?

Lizzi finished off her sandwich. "What do you do for food?" The moment she asked it, she knew it was a stupid question. "Sorry."

Elion smiled. "That's all right. By not paying rent, I've got plenty of money for everything else. In fact, I've been saving most of my salary in hopes of being able to put in higher bids on leases." His countenance fell. "After all, it won't be for much longer. Maybe another couple of months?" He looked to the photograph next to his computer.

He must miss Marla very much.

Lizzi stared at the remains of Elion's sandwich. "I'll keep your secret."

"And I'll keep yours."

She stiffened. "My secret?"

"I don't know what it is, but I can see you have one." He edged the rest of his food her way.

Her hand slid that unfinished sandwich off its wrapper. "Bring me breakfast tomorrow and I'll tell you all about it."

She logged into her computer. "So, work-wise. What are we up to?"

♀

The problem with engineering microg 21A-B's filaments for greater length was that their own weight cancelled out their lifting capacity. So much for solving the heavy bottom problem. Every single one of their lab tests failed.

Lizzi and Alice spent the rest of the day brainstorming possible adjustments to 21A-D. For once, Lizzi had a good brainstorming session, thanks to Elion's sandwich. Still, when Alice had to leave for the school run, all they had come up with were some rather silly ideas.

Lizzi handed her work over to the next shift and

returned home to her overpriced studio apartment.

In a city of this size, there were good streets and bad streets. Lizzi's street was considered one of the bad ones, but she didn't mind. The over-expensive city rents drove all but the well-employed out. Lizzi's neighbours were hardworking and rarely home. She knew most of them by sight, if not by name. Newly-wed or nearly dead, that was her neighbourhood.

The young professionals moved in when they won a bid on a cheap lease. These soon moved out as marriage and promotion brought greater financial freedom. The older folk must have been living here for decades. If this was all they could afford when rent was much lower, before the boom, no way they would be able to move to something better.

After her conversation with Elion, she looked at her neighbours anew. How many of them were subletting? No one would ever confess something like that. What did each of them pay for their lease?

Lizzi came home to a cold apartment in the dark. She didn't bother looking in the empty fridge; that had been turned off for several months. No television, no computer, nothing but a bed to welcome her.

Last month she had committed a crime she was not proud of. One morning she snuck in her bed sheets and washed them at work in the laundry facility meant for lab coats. They had been too big for her bathroom sink, and she didn't want to waste the water in her shower.

The milk she had gulped down at the end of her shift sat better in her stomach, now that it had a sandwich for company.

As she lay in the dark, awaiting sleep to overcome her, she pondered on her beloved microorganisms. Poor little things, flung out into the wilds of the Venusian weather. Would they fly up into the cold of space, or would they be dragged down to crushing depths, burned to death?

She dreamt that night of sunscreen and of toast that always landed butter-side-down.

♀

Hunger and hope woke Lizzi the next morning, as did the seeds of an idea in her head. Anticipation of a genuine breakfast fuelled her legs as she forewent public transport on her way to work. Almost as much as food, she missed the comfort and speed of the subway.

She found Elion in the lab with a bag of schmeared bagels and a cup of juice.

"Slow down," he admonished as she gulped down the juicy goodness. The occasional orange in the fruit bowl never compared with a good old juice.

Elion nibbled at a bagel. "So, what's this secret of yours?"

She waved away his question as she finished her juice. "In a moment. I think I figured out a way to save the microgs."

Once the juice hit her system, her stomach woke up with the promise of more nutrition. She pulled a bagel apart and stuffed it in her mouth. "Sorry," she said around soft, chewy bagel. "I promised you a secret."

After swallowing, she presented her plan. The food restored her courage. "The rent on my apartment went up. Because of that, I can't afford food." She took another bite of bagel. How good it was.

Elion studied her. "How long?"

"Few months."

Her stomach stretched. Elion was right; perhaps she should have slowed down.

He rubbed his finger along the edge of the bagel. "So what have you been eating?"

Heat suffused her face. "Anything I can find. Mostly company milk and fruit from the fruit bowl in the staff room, when they remember to stock up."

Elion's jaw dropped. "Expired yoghurt from the staff fridge?"

She nodded. Company policy required every item of food in the staff fridge to be marked with the date it was placed in the fridge. Anything left in the fridge after a week was thrown out. The cleaners came by at 5:00 in the afternoon. Lizzi checked the fridge at 4:55. Most people were diligent about their lunches, alas.

Elion leaned back in his chair, his bagel forgotten. "How long did you expect to live like this?"

Lizzi shrugged. She'd had no plan, nothing beyond where her next meal was coming from. Her future was non-existent, until now.

She leaned over and placed her hand on Elion's. "I have a problem and you have a problem. I think we can solve each other's problems."

Elion raised an eyebrow.

Lizzi drew a deep breath before her courage could flee. "I am willing to sublet my apartment to you."

He blinked. She rushed on, snatching at her ebbing courage. "It's not much, but it's a permanent address. Marla can come over and get a job. You'll be together. It'll only be sixteen hundred a week, less than what you were bidding for—"

He pulled his hand out from under hers. "And what will you do?"

Oh dear. There went her courage. "I..." Maybe this wasn't such a good plan after all. "I thought I'd—" how to say it? "I could do the homeless thing for a little while." Her voice trailed off. "If you could show me how."

He scooted his chair back, a hand over his mouth. Elion said nothing for a while.

Lizzi squirmed. Was he going to reject her?

After a resigned sigh, he said, "Do you know how hard it is living homeless?"

No, she didn't. But, "One little thing goes wrong in my life, and I'll find out soon enough."

Ah, there was a little bit of courage left in her tank after all. It swelled up. "At least this way, I've got a safety net. How long would it be? Three months? Six months? Long enough for Marla to get a job, and you could raise your bid on leases, and I could save up some extra money..." It sounded like such a good plan in the middle of the night.

Elion shook his head. "What if you are found out?"

"Why would they find me out? I've got my name on a lease."

"But what about me? What about Marla?"

"Nobody will ever know." Her heart thumped hard in her chest. He had to say yes.

Silence fell between them. Elion took another bite of his bagel, setting it back on the bench. "What if HR compare addresses?"

Ah. She hadn't thought of that.

Elion rose from his chair. "I've got to think about it. When's rent due?"

"Every two weeks." She couldn't meet his eyes. "Thank you for breakfast."

So much for that.

What was it like to live homeless?

♀

For the most part, 21A-D survived just fine in the Goldilocks Zone of the Venusian atmosphere. But once they became heavy with carbon chains, just before cell division, they sank down into the uninhabitable zone to perish.

Elion had left his unfinished bagel. Lizzi claimed it for her lunch. Even with her heart heavy, the bagel brought a moment of joy to her afternoon.

They might not be able to design the microgs to float when bottom-heavy, but what if they helped them along?

With a bit of input from Alice, Lizzi designed a concept of a balloon basket, similar to the weather balloons that monitored Venusian weather. These could hold the microgs, allowing them free access to all the carbon dioxide they could consume, yet catch them when they fell.

After cell division, 21A-D was light enough to float back up.

She posted her idea to the team wiki and returned to her cold, dark apartment.

Maybe she should have experimented with sleeping in the staffroom instead?

The next morning she ran into John but not Elion. "I thought your idea had merit," John said before he left. As for his lab partner: "He left early this morning."

Was Elion all right?

Her answer came when she logged on to her computer. Elion had added comments poking multiple holes in her idea—namely, it was too small-scale, and too expensive considering the global distribution of 21A-D.

As the tears welled in her eyes, she saw a new idea in the wiki. Elion's idea.

Forget the floating balloons. He suggested electrostatic micronets to harvest any 21A-D that had dropped. Do collection sweeps at certain altitudes, then restore the microgs to the proper levels once cell division had taken place.

Now, why hadn't she thought of that?

She stared at her screen for so long, the words lost their meaning. But not their merit. Before she left for the evening, she marked it as an idea worth exploring further.

♀

The next morning there was no sign of Elion, but he left a breakfast bar and a sticky note on her keyboard. The breakfast bar she saved for later. The note said,

"Conditional yes."

Conditional? For the rest of the day, she wondered what conditions Elion would request.

Lizzi and Alice sent a list of specs to the engineering department regarding a prototype micronet light enough to float at seven atmospheres and withstanding 65 Celsius.

Lizzi rejected the idea of sleeping at work that night. If Elion agreed to sublet, she wouldn't be sleeping in her own bed for quite some time.

Before she left, she penned a simple note for Elion's keyboard: "I'm listening."

♀

Elion found her the next morning as she raided the staff fridge for milk. The fruit bowl had been filled the night before. Lizzi snuck a couple of apples into her pockets and noshed on the largest banana in the bunch. Fruit made milk more tolerable as a food.

"So I was thinking," he said without preamble, a coffee cup in his hand, "have you ever heard of hot bunking?"

Lizzi topped her mug with pure milk before handing the jug to Elion.

He added the traditional slurp and sipped at his coffee. His sigh announced its perfection. "It's an old navy trick. When a submarine has more crew than bunks, they sleep in shifts."

Lizzi's mug froze halfway to her lips. "Surely you're not suggesting..."

He grimaced. "Well, not sharing the same bed, per se. I was thinking more like a roommate-type deal."

"Elion. My apartment isn't a one-bedroom apartment. It's a one-room apartment. Studio-style."

He sipped his coffee. "I know. But I also know what it's like to be homeless. I honestly cannot put you in such a position.

"You must have a safe place to sleep." He glanced around then leaned in closer. "You might think my living homeless is glamorous, but it's not. Every time I slept in public, even here in the staff room, I fell asleep with fear in my heart. Would I be robbed as I slept? Would I be beaten, abused?" A shudder of memory shimmied across his countenance. "I was lucky that I had a locker here to keep my worldly possessions. The second time I slept at the university, I woke up to find my bag stolen. Now, when I go out into the world, I leave my wallet here. I take only enough money for my daily needs, and my keycard to get back into work."

He cradled his mug close. "Home is more important than you know. It is the place you can rest when you're too heavy from the world and know you are safe. As much as I want that, I cannot completely take that away from you.

"Marla and I, we'd like to rent your bed and borrow your shower. But we'll only pay one thousand two hundred. Marla told me, that should you accept our offer, that we would buy you either a new couch for your bed, or one of those nice oriental screens for privacy."

Lizzi took another bite of banana. His offer was less than the true rent. Lizzi would be paying two hundred for the privilege of sleeping on a couch in a one-room apartment.

On the other hand, it would mean she would get to eat again. To be lifted from the darkness of starvation was motivation enough.

"Deal." Lizzi held out her hand to shake upon it. "When would you like to move in?"

A smile of delight spread across his face. "How about in a half-hour? I am already packed." He gestured to his duffel bag. From his pocket he pulled a wad of notes. "Here's a thousand now. I can get you more on payday."

Lizzi looked at the money in her hand. When was the last time she saw so much cash?

One thing was for sure. Today's lunch, and every lunch

for the rest of the week would be deli sandwiches, done just right. Nothing wrong with sleeping on the couch. From her purse, she pulled her housekey. "You might want to make a duplicate."

He pocketed the key. "Oh, you'll be pleased to hear what the supervisory committee said about your ideas."

"What?"

A secret grin played about his face. "You'll see when you check in to the wiki."

Her hand curled about the money. "I'll check it out after I've had some lunch."

WHEN WE WERE IN THRALL TO VENUS

Deborah Walker

We are not grounded.

Half a hundred kilometres above the surface of Venus, we soar. In her alien scripture. We inhabit a lightweight ceramic pod swinging from cables attached to an inflated polybenzoxasole balloon. Underneath our living quarters, hangs the Pegasus escape pod. We constantly think about escape.

We ride above the cloud bank, an impenetrable smog. Like angels we inhabit the heavens. Below is Venus, with her metal-melting heat, with her crushing atmosphere. Abysmal Venus, skin surging with cataclysmic forces, raging, spewing sulphur, plumes to add to the smog of the sky.

We move with the century winds, every four days we circle her.

And we watch her remotely, through squat machines. It feels like an intrusion. She should be veiled from our eyes.

We look on Venus, see her, burning, burning. We know she is beautiful. And we know that we will never know her, never walk on her surface.

She is so close, blistering bright, but she keeps us distant by her very nature. We want her. But we cannot have her, unless we utterly change ourselves.

We are not grounded. We are in a state of unease.

♀

Alma is the captain. She insists that we sit down each twelve hours together, to eat. She mothers us, missing her children. How easily we slip into our roles. We eat the tasteless rations while talking of the food we cannot eat: goat curry on a bed of rice and peas, sashimi delicately anointed with wasabi, avocadoes oozing and ripe, sour cream smooth and cloying to offset the fire of chili. We talk about food too much. The memories of food are a link to a world months ago. We talk about what we cannot have. We talk about our hunger.

Afterwards we sit and concoct wild schemes. Would it be better to terraform Venus, or venaform ourselves? Could we walk with silicate skin, eyes closed to her incandescence?

♀

A month we have lived here. Everything became mundane too quickly. And then the sickness started. She was more than our study; she was our obsession.

Verticordia is fluid as plasma. One moment positive, the next sunk into a depression. She says, "This place is both routine and marvellous. It is: wild and tame, strange and familiar, yesterday and tomorrow, back and forwards, to and fro, morning and evening."

The air we breathe is recycled though each other's lungs. Held for a lingering moment. We rebreathe each other's experience.

"Everything is everything," says Verticordia. "Everything is too intimate."

We scoop carbon dioxide and nitrogen from the atmosphere. We extract hydrogen from the acid rain. We make the air we breathe. We make the air that supports us.

"I always feel like I'm going to fall," says Felix. Despite the near Earth gravity, our steps fall hesitant onto the smooth floors. Felix lingers at the air lock, her long fingers almost touching the levers. "I wonder..." She does not have to say more. Strange compulsions inhabit us. We should not speak of them. To give them voice would be to give them power.

There are five of us. Who will be the first to fall?

♀

We experiment to find the ideal altitude. Up and down we go, by adjusting the bladders in the balloon. We adjust the stabilisers, riding the thermals.

We try to rationalise. We try to think as we've been taught.

She is: she is a rock and heat. She is Earth's near twin.

No. She is herself. Mysterious. Terrible and beautiful.

Because she holds us distant, in thrall to her, half a hundred kilometres away. Because she sets the parameters of our existence. Because she forces us to submit.

We love her, and we hate her.

♀

Eryx stalks the corridors, heat inhabits her. She touches our faces, brushes against us. We think she's possessed. Alma cautions her in whispers, "No more," she says.

Eryx's hand brushes against Alma's throat.

Alma, cat-like, jumps away.

Excess heat is dissipated by superstats at the end of flying tethers.

♀

We are different here. We are not human. Imagine everything taken away. Imagine taking away everything. Unanchored we are, and strange. While fires like hell burn below us, we walk light footed.

♀

Our days are filled with tasks to occupy our minds. At night we speak in whispers of our fears, our compulsions. In the small places, where we've learnt that we're not observed.

♀

It was inevitable.

♀

This aerostat habitat is the precursor for a hamlet, a village a city that will never come.

We should have told them. The men and women we'd worked with for years to get us here. Who spoke to us every day. But they were not us. They were not in thrall to her.

♀

"It will get better," we told ourselves. "We will acclimatize. This feeling will fade."

Yet it did not. Moment by moment we become Venus.

We are Venus Felix. We are Lucky Venus.

We are Alma Venus. We are Mother Venus

We are Venus Murcia. We are Venus of the Myrtle

We are Venus Erycina. We are the Fertile Venus of Eryx.

We are Venus Verticordia. We are Venus the Changer of Hearts.

And She is Venus Victrix. She is Venus the Victorious. We knew that when Felix finally opened the airlock and fell to her.

♀

For a moment we wonder if we all will fall. But then Venus releases us. We're no longer aspects. We become ourselves.

We turn to the consoles. We would be going home soon.

Back to earth. Venus is a sickness. She held us in thrall. She did not let us go until she had her taste of us. Venus is a sickness. And back on Earth, we will still long for her.

THE LAST TRANSIT OF VENUS

EM Edwards

*"In the cities, air and food were foul, and you had no idea what
came down in the rain."*

New Venusia is a city out of time. Open to all, a welcoming goddess spread out across King George Island but kept chaste behind a curtain of rain and mist and now distance from the centre of things, a triple headed guardian past which few penetrate. As ports go it's rarely approached by sea. Which is fine with the salties and the blooms of jellyfish who patrol the lagoon. The big reptiles lay clutches in the shadows of derelict cranes, hump their antediluvian bodies past warehouses whose metal roofs have pitted into lacework under the acrid rain. It's not its age, or Venus, old, that gives the port its name and the city its timeless character. They didn't get there, of course. No one will—one more transit forever out of reach to those watching below. The last commercial colony on Mars is twenty years dust and bodies which will never be buried. The eponymous bay beside which the city has grown old is all that remains of such Olympian dreams, that and their link in the resource trade out of the interior of the continent which flows north and east and rises and falls on pillars of flame.

Veska stands waiting for the vessel to alight. She shares the covered platform only with the morning, the city at her back and still asleep. The dead harbour lies at her feet. The visitor she's expecting hasn't come for a fanfare so she stands, solitary.

It's not much to see at first but she traces the path the transport makes from the direction of Águila Islet. Burning low over the clouds, clawing at them with rosy fingers and then through them, rent, the vessel blunt nosed and early as it banks. Veska's earlier still, having read more into the communiqué than it said. She has had no sleep but feels no tiredness.

It kicks up a localized typhoon of fog and bad smells: petrochemical reek, mudflat, formaldehyde and MCHM, the taints of precious metal processing and human waste coat her mouth as the transport incises a half-circle over the settlement. Its wings are stubby and downswept. The city may sleep but it rarely rests. New Venusia's nocturnal breath helps to keep the sky gravid. Veska wonders how many eyes have seen the vessel burst through it. The transit jet emits the unmistakable growl of war as its rotors readjust; for all its bulk it sets down light on extruded feet.

A hatchway opens and a lone operator is spat out, sweeps the landing zone with something that traces multiple red lines through the mist. He or she steps back inside, then a tight wedge bursts forth around Veska's visitor who moves hunched against the rain and under the weight of professional paranoia. Lithe figures clutching weapons cordon him from her sight.

No doubt they'd have preferred full combat drones but the local governance for all its laxness and nominal impartiality in the wars which the continent feeds with raw materials, has a ban on the things. Doesn't mean their visitors will abide by it, or that it can be enforced. New Venusia has fallen on hard times.

Which is why Veska stands here on show before the dawn. The personage doesn't care who greets them of course, nor would he notice if it was someone else. But she does and there are those in the city who would so here she is and it takes her knowledge of this to place a welcoming smile on her lips.

I hope the flight was uneventful, she says. But he's not interested. They don't exchange names. He's taller than she expected having seen him bent at a distance against the hissing rain; he towers over her. Looking down, his face is craggy and sunburnt by the deserts of the equator. His eyes an indeterminable shade behind the worming of information and uplink, they don't meet her own anyway, save to look past her and the covered platform with the same disdain.

Let's get inside, he grunts and that's what it is, a noise that he makes in his throat and he too, she supposes for all his swagger, is no more than that. Another soldier who thinks himself a conqueror, or perhaps the real thing. It hardly matters out here. Let him have what he wants so long as they get what they need.

He's running a hand across his shaven pate wiping away the rain and not pausing as she leads him to the steps and then to the lift and down a passageway and out the door, to her own transportation, a swarm of lesser members of his caste ranging ahead and behind in sister vehicles identical to their own. It makes him feel important, perhaps, but she doubts he's fool enough for it to make him feel safe. But safe he is. New Venusia for all the rise and fall of fortunes elsewhere knows when it's licked and what hand it must now press to its lips if it is not to be forced to do the same with the boot.

We could get some breakfast if you like, she say—but can see the refusal form on his face before he voices it, and he sees her register it and so ends up saying nothing; she continues, Never mind then, we'll go straight to the facility. I'm sure you want go over the agreement. Inspect the goods. Get up to speed with the most recent data we've had transmitted down from Luna.

Not here, he says; and she sees his hesitation as he looks over his entourage and her and out into the city. There is a sense of abandonment which Veska hopes is masked by the hour. Empty storefronts. Low slung, sixty-storey hyphaecologies shrouded in extreme weather proof cladding. A few stone buildings nearer the port mimic an antiquated style popular in the flush of new wealth over two centuries ago. But the factories are unlit. Tenement balconies closed in and closed off, hung with wind-borne trash but never laundry as they pass. Despite signs of a large population, you wouldn't know it to look at New Venusia this morning. He sees all this without seeing it, Veska observes. He's more nervous than he'd care admit, or else farther down the tree of decision making than he is comfortable revealing so wants his uncertainty unpacked in private. On this point they can both agree. If Veska is calm it is because she doesn't have a choice other than to trust the untrustworthy factions they've suborned.

This man is their agent, if not one of their commanders, and if he wasn't equally made nervy and rawboned over the stakes raised by his presence here, Veska and the others would know that their secret had been sold and they with it. There would be contrails right now over the ocean, orange fists tearing apart the cloud-cover as ugly shapes break the back of the horizon and rain down displeasure on the port city of New Venusia, a city which is only nominally a port these days, and which as far as Veska is concerned, only extant for the seeing off of one remaining convoy. Two, if you count the envoy though she doesn't.

But there were wars, endless wars, the race of mortals having been locked out of the heavens by their promethean children and their ploughshares turned back into swords to fight over ownership of a dying prison. You couldn't get a thing into orbit these days, let alone to Luna, without collusion.

So here she is sitting with a tiger in the backseat, showing it the sights, pointing out her quaint foggy village. Hoping it won't eat her alive on the strength of promising it a new set of teeth. No doubt the warlord or the messenger, whichever he is, thinks her and her city as dopey as force-fed geese. The yellow in his eyes Veska knows is just information, a sea of it, brighter than the one threaded with oil and algae and dying jellyfish and plastic that bathes the great ocean-going reptiles and further erodes the pilings. But it gives him a hint of menace and deification in the enclosed confines of the car that is unsettling. Their vehicle moves smoothly through the streets, requires no driver but knows the way unfailingly. Veska is glad—her hands are shaking.

They haven't passed any people and have seen only a handful of distant vehicles not a part of their group, moving through the weather. His soldiers in the car with them might as well be statues for all the sense of individual life they emit. Now a white building little more than a parking structure looms. Tires splash through the puddles.

As they slink into the garage and then circle deeper, doors trundling shut closing off each level behind them like the mechanical walls of Ílium, Veska relaxes. A little.

We're here, she says and they get out. Engines steam and their breath as well. Shan and Emmanuelle greet her, familiar faces among a skeleton crew of genii loci summoned from the darkness.

How are you, Doctor Veska? asks Shan.

Good. Everyone's well at home. And you?

I'm fine, says the ex-miner, but she doesn't look it. Not a bit. None of them do but then they're all former workers, nearly all of them women, from the interior mostly, their lungs full of carcinogens and their immune systems holed by years of heavy metal poisoning that has gone too far to be reversed. She looks, Veska thinks, worse than death: like one actively dying. But her smile is bright and warms Veska through as they press cheeks, and so too do those smiles on the faces of the others who stand about joking and laughing quietly in the bubble of their shared mission, genuine and true. The personage's bodyguard are not impressed. She addresses them and the envoy.

From here on commander, you'll have to take a reduced number, Veska says, trying for the lightest touch she can manage though her concern is for them, really, not for herself. She wants their visitors to be agreeable for their own sake. She looks at the women and men, more of the latter than the former, who have stepped out of the cars, eyes lost behind wraparound shades, clutching their combat rigs protectively as if she's suggested they extract their molars. They're all bigger than her. They could take apart anyone in the room without scuffing their boots.

Our security detail will be happy to kept you updated— but from here, she says. Commander, if you'll pick a smaller group we can proceed to the lower levels. She will bend on this point of course if she has to, but she hopes she'll not need to. She will fall on it too, if that is what it takes. Desperation is not always a weakness sometimes it is a strength.

He nods. She suspects he hasn't thought much of their protocols but hasn't judged them a danger either. Contempt is itself a useful aegis. Half his group are left behind to cool their heels with the cars. Another group is brushed off farther in when their augmentations get in a noisy argument with the facilities' countermeasures. All so smoothly.

At last they're in the inner sanctum. It's him and her plus three of his lieutenants and none of her own. She's glad for that. It's just a room, likely used for breaks by some of the staff or for storing things like cups or cleaning supplies and has the feel of only intermittent usefulness. Someone has left a mop leaning in a corner. The envoy doesn't seem to understand at first why they've stopped here, then tightens his jaw muscles and sits down.

But what is Veska to say? That they don't have a command centre, that they don't even have a command? Not here anyway. To the human everything is human-shaped. To the followers of Mars everything is a sword. What is important in this place, isn't for their eyes. What is dangerous is what isn't on display. He's not going to see it and Veska isn't about to tell him that either.

Here are the newest vectors, the numbers and the payload, their telemetry, she says, and she passes him the hard figures on a tablet. He seems puzzled if not outright amused at something that isn't just mainlined into his synapses. But the facility this far in has its special Faraday cage in place, so that's what really makes it a sanctum, nothing else. The rest is just a couple of chairs hastily found and arranged, a table, and some refreshments which might, Veska suspects, have already been there like the mop. The coffee isn't fresh and the rolls are definitely stale. Not that her visitor touches either. She does, though. Helps herself twice. It's been a long night, an early start, and the day promises to be, if the promises made elsewhere are kept, one without visible bottom. She enjoys the bitter brew and dry pastry like it's her last meal on Earth.

And the weapons? he asks. He doesn't use that word, but the words he uses mean the same thing. It is all weapons to him. What the weapons are, or what they are called, hardly matters to Veska.

She and the others are used to handing over the raw materials. They no longer worry about what others will do with them, and Veska says, Yes, we'll see those next but I need confirmation that you understand our requirements here first. Agreement that the factions can do this.

The contempt rises in his face buoyed on a surge of incipient violence but he waves at Veska and the room, and the tablet. Yes, yes, he says, and Veska can see he means it even if he is already bored with this end of the conversation, which revolves around things which are not to the best of his understanding, at all useful as weapons and so instantly he devalues and distrusts them and her in the same impulse. The x, y and z teams, he says—or something of that sort, and Veska feels a similar lack of ability to focus on the details he spits out, his burnt face growing animated as the data streams behind his eyes truncated and looped as they are by the limitations of their special environment—are already in place. We can guarantee safe passage for the launch, but no longer than that. Once you achieve LEO you're on your own. This and that difficulties, and this and that contingencies, he continues on, while Veska's head spins and her face flushes. She'll review the files later, but for now she grips the table and tries to breath in a steady manner.

Excellent. Fine. That will be satisfactory, says Veska, hoping these are appropriate responses.

She has thumbed the tablet on the table. He does, with absentminded reluctance, the same. Already greater forces have begin to gather. Veska imagines she feels a shiver of dread and excitement and something else—hope?—vibrate up through the concrete and wire mesh that honeycombs the room. It rises through her feet or else it arises *in her* and is sent downward, a signal that will soon race and match those flying about the complex triggered by that dual thumbprint as soon as they leave the room.

The personage doesn't even notice her excitement. He's thinking just about the weapons and the asymmetrical face of their bargain. Veska silently agrees with his judgement, even if he doesn't understand the bargain he's made. Doesn't understand that he and the factions have sold their birthright, all of their birthrights if you look at it this way, for a cup of porridge seasoned with retro sequenced bacilli from the Plague of Justinian, low gravity bred small pox, bits of salvaged machine hardware left behind on the Moon and viral smart bombs they've designed themselves from the remains. They're just *things*, for all their deadly glitter. Trinkets and beads and old blankets.

Veska feels a twinge of guilt but it passes. Sowing more death among the few or the many matters little when the alternative is the extinction of all. They've handed down the orbital vine some impressive new toys for the people still playing at war on the surface of the old world. The Moon hangs unseen above them, a last foothold on the edge of an endless night. They've done impressive work up there and if the factions knew the full extent, Veska is unsure what would happen. Nothing good.

But out in the Kuiper Belt ships not their own blaze routes through Sol system. They move like schools of silvery squid beaming a constant encrypted flow of chatter that has nothing of the human in it. Left behind, discarded and told in no uncertain terms to stay out of the rest of the local real estate, humanity doesn't even bother looking up anymore. The problem is, property values here on Earth are never going to recover. Not in their species' lifetime, or in whatever's comes next and now that they've made certain of that, it is only a race to see who can burn down the homestead first and most spectacularly. Veska knows all this and ticks it off in her head, a sequence that firms her courage where once it made her weep.

If they're going to make it, it will be out there. If they're going to have a chance to repossess the dream too long denied them by their greatest, singular mistake, they'll have to travel farther. To leap past where they've been barred from crawling. Farther than the transit of Venus, farther than the slow growing airlessness of Mars and the asteroids noisy with low-frequency radio waves and bursts of x-ray and gamma serenades of pure mathematics. To put their hope in a goddess, not a god of war. They tried fighting for the right to range, and lost, and now back on the reservation they're losing another war. A campaign of steady and willful attrition, want and manufactured pestilence, famine and lethal ennui.

Are we done here? The warrior looks anxious to leave the room that so limits him. His lieutenants are staring at Veska who holds her cooling cup in both hands.

Veska tries not to let her startlement show. Or her joy. She was drifting there, far out beyond Low Earth Orbit, and her heart pounds and her face burns upon reentry.

Sorry, yes. I have clearance to release the items to you now, commander. Come have a look and then we'll get them on their way to your transport, she says. I'm sure your team is tired of waiting upstairs. The complex is mostly empty now.

I'd recommend a tour of the city but I'm afraid the weather isn't likely to get better. There's a storm moving in across the Bransfield Strait that I'm told will make landfall at Cape Melville within the hour. We'll have to make do—and we will—but unless you want to stay until the launch which is our best shot for having something resembling favourable conditions, it will be more of the same dark cloud you arrived under. I know a place in one of the waterfront hotels that does really good farm raised calamari; the chef, she's a friend of mine.

We'll go, he brushes her off. I didn't come here for sightseeing, he says matter-of-fact without a trace of humour as far as Veska can tell. New Venusia has never been famous for its sights. Or for that matter, its cuisine. Sulphuric rain and heavy metal runoff doesn't encourage fishing.

They're on their way to the upper level where the boxes are waiting. They've only come down this deep because they had to be certain. Certain that the deal they've struck with the devil will stick, certain that if it didn't they could kill everyone in the room, in the whole complex if necessary, to keep the data on the tablet from leaving. Layers of concrete and automated systems to scrub wandering eyes and ears other than their own that might have hitched a ride. That's why Veska volunteered. They had argued about it at home, her wife crying when she left her in the pre-dawn gloom still rumpled from a sleepless night, and repeatedly, days before with others on the team weighing in, angrily and hotly, but she holding firm until her seniority prevailed. If they were going to risk it all on this throw, she was going to hold the dice herself and fall with them as they tumbled.

Veska feels life return to her, the full spectrum bursting forth after weeks and months and years of dulling toil, stress, despair and reversals, stepping free of these last few hours stooped under a shadow. The sweat on her lip is as cold as the blood in her veins is hot and the latter pounds in each temple like a bell struck by a priestess. What they have done here may yet fail but it cannot now be undone.

Rising through the levels she both sees things minutely and not all. It's a blur of fine details which sparkle as if under magnification, individual snowflakes swirling together to cause whiteout conditions in her mind as they gather up the missing toy soldiers the personage has left scattered behind: clumps of men and women standing in wide industrial spaces empty of everything but them. The industry that they've housed for so long, decades of work, decades longer of planning, have ceased. The fruits of that labour, that sweet vine that now uncurls towards the stars far above the thick clouds and sheet-lightning, is swollen, ripe. Ready to be plucked and sent tumbling into the absolute cold betwixt earth and moon. They have the means now, to make that leg of their journey, just the tiniest part, in relative safety. Veska feels like the shade of Herakles left behind in the Underworld, though her future living self has no assurance she won't join her there.

She sees tears in the corners of Shan's eyes as the cars are started. The others working their meagre detail are more pragmatic or else lack the moisture. Deadman switches are surreptitiously powered down and the weight of their collective death sentences settle back unpardoned upon their shoulders. They have paid the price already, these women and handful of men, in pits and in refineries, in tenements and in waste processing plants, and this is just the coin the ferryman demands for his services.

They'd have done it anyway, but Veska and the others know that to buy the same passage with force would have cost an exchange they'd have only paid if they had no other currency. Like the hidden death in the room they've recently left. Like the fallout with the factions that they'd have had to weather if their soldiers never returned from New Venusia, or without their representative or the gifts with which they have wooed them. Better to choose love, better to be a hierodule and give what was asked of them than another virtuous combatant.

She is happy, despite being poised between two states, only surprised that it has all come out so well. No doubt the factions think them dupes because the factions will want more, and it won't be long before the source is traced back to Veska and the others, but by that time, it won't matter. It will of course, matter, for those left behind in New Venusia but that's a price that the city has chosen to pay even if some of its citizens don't know it's been chosen for them.

There is, however, another surprise left for her. As they watch the cargo that her guilty mind neither wishes to visualize or have to itemize beyond the abstract, be packed away, the commander turns to her and grins, sly in his manner all of a sudden. The smile makes him look more tigerish.

Is it true? he asks her. Is it true that you're sending up not just colonists but a whole starship?

She is taken aback, seized by a lurching heart that swings pendulum like between pride and panic. The envoy is clear-eyed behind the data flows. She can see by the lights on her wrist he's not transmitting anything off the base and certainly not out of the city yet. There is no profit in it anyway. If it is a trap or an attempt to shock a confession out of her, it's too late. They've not really been secretive about this in the way that people who love weapons are secretive about the things they do, other than the weapons themselves which they're handing over to these men and women burnt by the sun over Africa and Brazil, by the bursts of specialized payloads dropped on the cities that glitter there or in the badlands that stretch both south and north from that narrow band of solar arrays and old money. But she's underestimated the man and perhaps the factions. They may have always understood, but either don't care or care just enough to let them get away with it.

Not exactly, but yes, she says. Veska thinks of the puzzle that the components represent. All those pieces. Not a ship. But parts of it. They've broken so many rules. A lot has been done where it can be done in real privacy, up on Luna and in orbit. They need to travel light. But they're sending their share from New Venusia too. Cold materials. Warm bodies, frozen down to inanimacy true, but destined to go farther than Luna in their icy sleep. Engines designed and tested for the crucial step of reentry into a gravity well and an atmosphere. Plants and genes and mission crucial personnel. Like Veska. And her heart leaps again.

Inanna is it? And now Veska feels a splinter of that deep chill pierce her breast, ice crystals floriate in her blood. Perhaps she should have pushed the panic button that sealed off the room those many floors down and which would have flooded it with an unsurvivable atmosphere of pathogens and finally, radiation. One of the moons there, says the envoy firmly, You've named it Ésagila. It is not a question. He's just reminding her that information is a weapon and he's not above or beneath using it. Will they let you? he asks.

Who, the factions? says Veska. She still hasn't raised her defenses and she can't seem to deflect him. Though now it is her chance to pretend slyness. He doesn't mean those who might oppose their clandestine alliance here on Earth. But colder intelligences that wait up above.

That's your job, isn't it? she says, still fumbling. That's why we're paying you— Veska only narrowly avoids adding the word off.

No, he says, You know that's not who I'm talking about. Among his caste it is almost a superstition to mention their name. The defeat was history before the commander took up the sword but like all soldiers he feels the shame of it keenly, even at a distance.

Now Veska is overcome by understanding. They aren't going to stop them because the factions don't think there's a reason to try. Should they win through or be destroyed, it will be a provocation, or they hope. Despite the futility of it, there is more than one group on Earth that yearns for a renewed contest of wills. Veska could tell them such a gesture would be worse than worthless; here in New Venusia they know better than most. When the wave struck, they suffered. The scars of which can still be seen if you know where to look.

It will take a long time, he says—with a hint of admiration in his voice, if they let you past the belt, if you lot can survive the rigours of such a trip, and then the last set of doors are open and he says nothing more as they exit under a sky that is lower and more bruised than before.

But Veska has heard enough. Enough to know where they stand with each other; and that he doesn't know *everything*, obviously, doesn't know about the other things they've achieved up on the Moon. She tries not to let it show. If he did, they'd both likely be dead. Warriors can't resist possessing a weapon even if it's not meant to be used as one.

Veska sees him to the landing platform. The wind tears at her coat. They have left the pretense of speech back at the complex. Both wish to go home. She watches the subtly armoured figures retreat to their black hulled ship, oarsmen filing on who have traded their oars for built-in weaponry and reflexes faster than their thoughts. White-hot engines for sails, ripple the air with heat signatures. The commander pauses on the lip of the hatchway, she sees him across the distance mouth words which she later hears played back on a recording the listening devices ringing the field have captured: Good luck. We hope you make it.

She does too. Only days to go until she leaves New Venusia and its useless port and basking lizards behind. Not more than double that until she is sitting in a habitat looking back at the world she will have left forever. That view-among the last she'll see of Earth. But the one which will have come before both of these glimpses, will have been made on the final trip up out of the atmosphere that anyone is likely to make. It has taken the hoarded wealth of a hard working continent to deliver her and those who will travel with her, and all the scientific cleverness gathered on Earth's dead satellite to arrange it. They're spent; this desperate throw of their spear won't be repeated unless something more miraculous than the inevitable happens back here or out there in the system in their absence. And miracles are the province of deities not terrestrial life. If they have learned any lesson in the last two hundred years, or had it taught to them, it is this.

Veska has to hope their cast can escape the net of humanity's unwitting mistake, the cage that they made for themselves that has locked them to one hot, crowded planet, and its chill companion. Pray that Athene stands at their shoulder and not just their namesake.

Over the bay, named after a goddess of love whose face they have found seeded among the stars and given her name to, or one like it, Veska sees the transport turn the clouds golden; dreams in that moment of her own journey yet to come, of rising up, and then falling further still, on one last transit across the face of the Sun, and then whipped around it to hurl without sound past machine listening posts and the dead faces of planets that will never be theirs. But towards one which they will at last, at the end of their wandering, claim as their own.

THE LADY ANARCHIST CAFÉ

Lorraine Schein

I stopped by the Lady Anarchist Café one fine summer evening, and ordered a red pepper crêpe with black mushrooms and a Fizzy Lizzy. It was only open from twilight till dawn and it was fast approaching closing time.

The café was run by the descendants of Emma Goldman, Voltairine de Cleyre and Victoria Woodhull, so it was a fitting place to dine in for someone like me.

A mysterious woman in a large black and red hat came in and sat at my table. Her face was vaguely familiar, but I couldn't place it.

"Are you interested in the planet Venus?" she asked, glancing at me sharply from under her brim, then looking away.

"Yes, as interested as anyone here," I replied, taking a sip of my sizzling drink, stirring the popping foam with a swizzle stick shaped like a bomb's wick. "Why do you ask?"

"I am a recruiter for a colony of women soon to be established there. We are looking for settlers, those unsatisfied with what was done on the Moon."

"Ah yes, the disaster that is the Moon." The Moon had become an industrial wasteland run by greedy corporate men.

"And where on that bright planet will this colony be?"

"We have settled in the cloud-communes above Venus, over the craters that still bear women's names, continuing the ancient tradition. All the craters on that radiant but hellish planet (so beautiful from afar!) were long ago named after women, both famous and not."

She paused, rifled through her handbag and pulled out a long sheet of paper. "Here is a partial list," she said.

Abigail
Abika
Abington
Abra
Adaiah
Adamson
Addams
Adivar
Adzoba
Aethelflaed
Afiba
Afiruwa
Aftenia
Afua
Aglaonice
Agnesi
Agoe
Agrippina
Ahava
Aigul
Ailar
Aimee
Aisha...

She read through the entire list beginning with A and ending with Z. It took quite a while and my dinner grew cold.

"I didn't hear my name on your list," I said. She handed it to me.

"Then you must change your name. For example, I am from the Voltairine Cloud-Commune, which floats over the crater that bears her name. To join us, you would have to change your name to Voltairine 340, as we currently have 339 members. Come join my Cloud—be a Volt! We are named after the famous 19th-century anarchist, Voltairine de Cleyre—so we are called the Volts."

Then leaning forward, she said "Do you know who I am?"

I shook my head, still unsure.

"My name is Cassandra Cobb... You may have seen me on the zip news or seen the photos of my grandmother, Jerrie Cobb, one of the only women who qualified to go to the Moon in 1959. She had not been allowed to go, though tests results showed that females were more qualified for space: they could withstand isolation and stress better, and were lighter."

I remembered the image now—the woman pale-haired as the Moon, wearing her old astronaut uniform, standing in a group picture of all men beside her.

"But now I can do what my grandmother could not," she continued, "leave Earth, and take other women with me. As Voltairine herself once wrote, 'Let yourself go free!'"

♀

Of course I said yes. We stood up and she led me to the launchpad where the individual warp-twist jetpacks and astrosuits lay piled. It would take us five weeks to get to Venus, but it would be worth it.

Soon we were rising with the others. Hordes of women, like cities reorganizing skyward, a rocket-shaped outline of soaring women, with Cassandra at its helm.

We would colonize Venus with the granddaughters of the women flyers who had been denied the Moon and the ancestors of the radical women of all centuries.

As we drew closer to the edge of the Cloud, I could make out the purple and silver spiral against the black of the Goddess flag. Under this was the slogan: "Keep Venus for Women—Take Back the Light!"

Cassandra had explained that the Volts lived in an enclosed bubble community. They grew hydroponic vegetables on a collective farm run by the daughter of a former 1970s radical feminist. Other extremist groups lived in nearby clouds, or wanted to. A libertarian cloud-commune was getting ready to come up soon, and had reserved a nearby cloud zone, after negotiating with its current TAZ-Beyian neighbors.

We would dwell there happily in freedom—all madwomen, anarchists, descendants of spurned astronauts, neglected scientists. Our new home was lit by the pale radiance of Earth, its blue-green swirling luminescence finally left behind. Cassandra told us that at Earth-rise, the others would greet us as we landed, to celebrate our arrival.

♀

It's been 20 years since I first met Cassandra at the Anarchist Café. Our cloud on Venus turned out to be the only one that has remained free, because of our stubborn devotion to our beliefs and each other.

Now Mercury is a solar panel farm, and Mars is a hamburger plantation settled by McDonald's bondholders.
I have a granddaughter now, who has just graduated from the Interstellar Academy here.

I have told her my story many times, but she says she doesn't mind hearing it again. She was cloned with the slightly randomized DNA from my cells.

On the anniversary of Voltairine de Cleyre's birth, together we watch the celebration. Eerily beautiful, the red fireworks shoot off with Earth as their green backdrop, our own evening star.

She watches it with me, then turns and says, "I want to be like you, Gran, carry on the tradition."

"I'm glad to hear that," I say.

"I want to go even farther, to the most distant galaxies, to found new interstellar colonies for the Volts—past what our science says can be reached."

And I smile to myself thinking of what Voltairine said:

"Turn cloudward, starward, letting oneself go free, go free beyond the bounds of what fear and custom call the 'possible...'"

ADAPT OR DIE

Erin M Hartshorn

Venus was the last stand for unaltered humanity.
      Sienna stood on her balcony, staring out at the poisonous fogs, and mourned. It shouldn't have been this way. She had made the right decision at every step along the way. No decision would have changed this. None of hers, anyway.

♀

"The new exosuits have all the latest tech, even some that's not on the market yet!" Cherry burbled away as they headed west on I-80, her cornrows swinging in time to her speech. "Muscle enhancers, air filtration—Tom said they even have 'soup nodes' that build amino acids out of the gases. It'll be just like eating in the canteen."

Sienna made encouraging sounds while checking the traffic. There wasn't much this far west, but every now and then, a cop liked to play hide-and-seek, looking to score revenue off the speeders. Confident there was no one around, she accelerated. It was a long way yet to San Francisco, and then on to Jarvis Island and the beanstalk off the planet.

"You're not even listening!"

"Sure I am." Sienna cast her mind back to what Cherry had been saying. "You think you could get to like algae soup?"

Her sister sighed theatrically. "I knew you weren't listening. I *said* Tom wanted to know if he was going to see you again."

"He's going to be there when I drop you off, isn't he?"

"You're missing the point. He wants to *see* you. You know, like ask you out on a date?" Cherry leaned sideways in her seat and propped her feet up against the window. "You can be so clueless."

♀

Transit from Earth to Venus was slow. The first week, Sienna stared out the window a lot, but the view didn't really change once they had left Earth orbit. She could finally pick out some of the constellations she'd always had trouble with back home, but after a while, she might as well be staring at the wall.

When she'd succumbed to the inevitable boredom, the captain put her to work. "No one's dead freight on my ship. We got to carry food, water, and oxygen for you, you're going to make it worth our while."

After that, she alternated three shifts in the mess with two of maintenance and repairs. In her downtime, she studied the history of Venus, the UA Explorers, the separatists, and pretty much anyone else she could blame for where she was now. Back on Earth, she had thought she was well-informed. But she'd been looking at a single, very carefully edited view of the news.

Now she only wondered two things: why had it taken this long for things to go so wrong, and what would she do when she got to Venus?

♀

She'd expected driving in the Bay Area to be crazy, and San Francisco didn't disappoint her. When Sienna eventually found her way to the wharfs, she wondered whether it was worth looking for a parking space. Cherry could catch the transport to Jarvis without her, and fast goodbyes were the best, weren't they? Like ripping off a bandage and just letting the wound bleed.

"Don't even think about it," Cherry said. "If you don't want to date Tom, fine, but you *are* coming to the beanstalk with me."

"I never said otherwise." Sienna followed the signs directing her toward a parking garage. If she'd been thinking, she would have rented a car to drive out. Long-term parking was going to cost more than a rental would have, assuming any parking spots were available.

The spot she found, wedged into a corner, wouldn't have been legal anywhere else she'd been. "Get out and direct me."

"If I had my exosuit, I could pick up the car and put it there for you."

"You don't, so out, now."

There really wasn't enough room between the other cars—a tiny smart car and an immense Hummer—for her to get through. On the other hand, the smart car looked fairly mobile. She rolled down her window. "Think you can nudge that one over?"

Her sister looked at it doubtfully. "They've got the parking brake locked."

That wasn't enough to discourage Sienna. She set her own brake and got out of the car. "Grab the back end. I think we can do it together."

"You're crazy, you know that?"

Even though the car's frame was lightweight polymer, it took more effort to move than she'd expected, but they did manage. Then they parked their car, grabbed Cherry's gear and Sienna's overnight bag, and headed for the transport. Sienna tried not to feel guilty about the pickle the other driver would be in, getting their car out. Maybe they'd decide they had just misremembered which stall they were parked in.

Tom—Major Thomas Paine Garcia of the United American Explorers—was waiting for them by the gangplank leading to the ship. "I thought maybe you'd changed your mind." He winked at Cherry, then smiled and extended his hand to Sienna. "Glad you decided to come with her."

She took his hand briefly but didn't say anything. She had no intention of marrying a military man, and that's what the explorers were, even if it wasn't what they called themselves. Mars, Venus, and Enceladus might not have native populations, but there were protestors to subdue, as well as people from other continents to compete with. Fighting was part of the job.

♀

The orbital station above Venus was nothing like the one at the top of the beanstalk. It didn't have to be, since it had no tether. This station had started, like the ISS, as a scientific research station, with room to dock one ship—two if absolutely necessary, but the astronauts had to be willing to spacewalk to get inside the station.

From there, it had expanded, and by the time Napier City and Gabor had been built, Venus Station was almost a miniature city of its own. Of course, most cities didn't have hand-to-hand combat in the streets.

When the airlock door swung open, Sienna stood motionless and stared at the fighting in dismay. She'd fled Earth to get away from the separatists, battles, and anything which put her life in danger. It hadn't done a bit of good.

"You headed to Napier?" A woman's voice came from her right, but Sienna didn't turn to look. She was too busy trying to figure out what to do next.

"Hey, I said are you headed to Napier?" This time, the question was accompanied by a tug on her arm, and Sienna looked down at a petite woman whose skin was half a shade lighter than her own.

"Napier?" It *was* the biggest city on Venus, such as it was. It made as good a next step as any. "I guess I am."

"Great. My name's Dee." She stuck her hand out. "I've got a cloud-skimmer over this way. I'll even let you pilot it part of the way."

♀

Sienna found herself wishing she could speed up the transport ship as easily as she'd floored her car on I-80. The region around Jarvis Island—around any beanstalk—was a no-fly zone, so they had to travel by sea. Unfortunately, that meant more time for Tom to try to woo her. Out of places to hide from him, she ducked into the comms centre in time to hear the fateful announcement.

"San Francisco's under attack. We got out just in time."

"Under attack? By whom?" Sienna blurted the words, only realizing she wasn't supposed to be in the room when the comms technicians turned to look at her.

They looked back at each other, then one of them walked toward her. "I'm afraid you're going to have to leave, ma'am. If there's anything to tell you, the captain will do it."

She shrugged off the woman's hold on her elbow. "I'm sure I can find someone with a phone that will reach the mainland somewhere on this ship and get the news from outside. Why don't you save me the trouble and tell me what's going on?"

"Ma'am—" began the woman next to her, but the man who had remained by the terminal cut in: "We don't know. You heard exactly as much as we know—the city's under attack. We seem to be outside the radius of destruction and. with any luck, we'll get to Jarvis safely. We don't know who, we don't know why. I hope you brought enough luggage for a long stay on the island."

She stared at him, uncomprehending. "We're not going

back?" After they'd worked so hard to park the car, too.

The woman snorted. "Oh, sure. We're just going to sail right back to where there are bombs and who-knows-what-all going on because *of course* our ship would never be targeted in an attack."

Sienna wandered the passageways, trying to find her way back to the deck, to look toward San Francisco. California was over the horizon by now, though.

Tom found her there, leaning on the rail, peering into the past. "You've heard?"

She nodded without looking at him. "Do they know who it was yet?"

"Separatists." He leaned on the railing next to her. "My guess is they couldn't get to the beanstalks, so they went for visible targets instead."

"Not just San Francisco?"

He didn't say anything, and Sienna swallowed. Maybe she didn't want to know. After a minute, she said, "You're sure they can't get to the beanstalks?"

"After the rise of terrorists in the new millennium, nothing that big got built without safeguards, I'm sure."

Sienna wished she could be as confident as he sounded.

The skimmer slid through the murk, gliding down from orbit to Napier City. Behind them, Sienna knew, a battle was being waged on Venus Station. She nudged the throttle forward to put more distance between her and the warring factions.

"You arrived just in time for all the excitement." Dee slouched in her seat, scooching around to make herself comfortable. "We can go days without any visitors, and now everyone shows up at the same time."

"That wasn't exactly coincidence." Sienna settled back, sure the skimmer would alert her if another spacecraft came near. "You do know what happened on Earth, don't you?"

"Mmmm. I've heard rumors—probably more current than your news."

"So what have I missed?"

"You can't go back to Earth. It's cut off."

Her chest tightened, but with a nostalgia of pain. She didn't even know when she'd given up on going home again, only that at some point between launch and arrival here, she had started to think ahead to what she was going to do with her life on Venus.

"What are the immigration rules?" Sienna grinned at Dee, but Dee didn't smile back.

♀

They weren't the only ship stranded at Jarvis Island. Sienna didn't bother trying to sort out the chain of command or why any particular person was giving orders. When she was told she'd be barracking in her cabin on the transport because there wasn't enough space on the island, she didn't even protest. The only thing that stirred her from her lethargy was Cherry coming to say goodbye.

"You're still going up the stalk?" Sienna couldn't believe her sister was abandoning her in this refugee camp.

"I've got a job to do, and at least I'll have some space to do it in." Cherry looked around the cabin disdainfully, then looked back at Sienna. "I take it Tom hasn't come by yet?"

"Why are you so determined to fix us up?" Sienna hadn't missed Cherry's dismissive attitude toward her living quarters—as though Sienna had had a choice in the matter—but instead of answering what hadn't been said, she grabbed at something she could be legitimately annoyed with.

"That's not—you know, never mind." Cherry had her hand on the door latch, ready to leave, but she paused. "I'm glad you came to see me off. I wanted us to get a chance to hang out before I left, anyway, but with the attacks, at least I know you're safe here."

"At least until we run out of food."

"Why do you have to make this hard?"

Sienna sighed. "I'm sorry, Cherry, but it *is* hard. We're in a siege here. More ships might come in, but no one's leaving. Did you know I have a job now? I'm harvesting seaweed, which is going to be our new vegetable of choice. How long do you really think that's going to be sustainable?" She didn't wait for her sister to answer. "The truth is, this really is goodbye. You're probably not coming back from Enceladus, and even if you do, I'm not going to be here. No one's going to be here, unless the separatists have moved in."

"Gloom and doom much?" But Cherry took her hand from the door and sat down on the bed next to Sienna. "That's why Tom was going to talk to you. Not all the transports made it in. There's room on the mission if you want to come."

Sienna stared blankly at her sister. Go into space? Become military, even if they called themselves explorers? Or thrust herself into the middle of the conflict with the separatists, all the many flavours of which wanted different concessions and were willing to use different tactics to get them?

"I know it's not what you wanted from life, but it's a chance," Cherry said. "A better chance than you'll get sitting here on your ass."

"Lovely language." Her mockery was remote, automatic. She was still processing what Cherry had said, trying to figure out what she felt, thought, wanted to do.

Napier's main energy expenditure was maintaining neutral

buoyancy. The city floated at cloud level, about 60 kilometres above Venus's surface, which at least made the temperature comfortable, even if the chemistry was actively hostile. Sienna was given housing on the west side of the city, where she could watch the sun rise each day, the darkest red sunrise she'd ever seen. She was also given access to the section of the city's system outlining the laws of Venus in general and Napier City in particular. No one even pretended they were affiliated with Earth any more.

She fell asleep reading the rules on employment and woke to someone leaning on the door buzzer. Blearily, she stumbled to the door. "Yes?"

Dee said, "You haven't left your rooms since we got here. Have you even remembered to eat?"

Sienna blinked at her. She'd read something about food, communal dining maybe, if someone didn't want to cook for themselves (assuming they had the money to pay for real food to cook). It hadn't seemed important at the time, but now her stomach rumbled, and she was aware of the empty pit inside of her.

"I take it that's a no," Dee said.

"I slept. Can't think straight. Give me a minute or two to wake up, okay?"

Dee nodded toward the nearest chair. "You might as well sit down. Your body's not used to Venus yet, but we're going to fix that."

"My body? My *mind* isn't used to Venus yet." Sienna slumped into the chair Dee had indicated, then looked up, quizzically. "What do you mean fix it?"

Dee leaned against the door, looking as nonthreatening as anyone could when they've just promised to fix something that isn't broken. "Humans didn't evolve for life on Venus. We can—*we have to*—make some accommodations, like bringing in water from asteroids, but that's not enough to really adapt to life here."

"Adapt," Sienna said flatly. She knew what that meant;

biological changes, supplemental mitochondria that could metabolize the sulphur compounds in the air, and more.

"Don't I get a choice in the matter?"

"You came here of your own free will, but there's always a choice. You can adapt, or you can die."

♀

A week after Cherry and Tom had left for Enceladus, extra exosuits and all, bombers streaked overhead.

Sienna stood on the deck of the transport and watched them. "I thought beanstalks were no-fly zones!"

One of the crew sneered at her. "In case you missed it, most of the fighters on the island already left, and I wouldn't count on help from elsewhere. If there still is an elsewhere."

She stared at him uncomprehendingly. The bombers had to come from somewhere; that meant someone was still out there.

Bombs dropped; one hit the ship anchored next to them. After that, she didn't pay much attention to what anyone else was doing. Survival seemed more important than whether or not the crew were at their stations.

The transport was a target. Hell, the whole island was a target, but the beanstalk itself was probably the safest place to be—it had been built to survive extensive damage. Unless those bombers crashed directly into it, they probably couldn't harm it. Even if they did, they might not harm anything except their own planes.

She ran for the beanstalk.

People were running, screaming. Dirt erupted into the air, along with metal, Humvees, and other things Sienna didn't want to think about too carefully. She didn't—couldn't—focus on what was going on around her. All she could do was try to get somewhere safe.

Her legs burned from exertion, and sharp pains cut her

throat. She hadn't run since high school. At least she went to the gym; otherwise, she might not have managed as much as she did.

She dropped to a walk, staggering the last hundred yards or so to the base of the beanstalk. One of the jets was coming down. Maybe they wouldn't see her. But she couldn't think about that. She kept going, step after step.

Finally, the base of the stalk, and a car ready to go up. Just waiting for her, maybe. She didn't care; she was going to get away. And if there was a spacecraft at the top, she'd take it. She didn't care where it was going.

♀

Sienna stood on her balcony, staring out at the poisonous fogs, and mourned. It shouldn't have been this way. But if she'd stayed behind in San Francisco, or at Jarvis Island and the beanstalk, she'd be dead now, and if she'd gone with Cherry and Tom—well, she might not be dead, but it wouldn't have been any better than life here. An exosuit in the frozen hell of Saturn's moon or stuck aboard a ship orbiting above it, watching the reserves dwindling? Neither was a terrific option.

"Are you ready?" Dee's voice came from behind her, and Sienna turned away from the hot, red cloudscape to look at the other woman.

"Is this something I can ever be ready for?"

"I was."

Sienna nodded thoughtfully. "I suppose you were." Her sister and Tom, whatever he might have wanted to be to her, were gone forever. Earth, Venus, Enceladus—they would all develop separately now. Maybe in a dozen years or fifty or a hundred, representatives of each world would meet one another again. Would the people from Enceladus have new, shiny exosuits with even more functions? Or would they have altered their biochemistry to match their new home—as she must now do?

"I'm ready." She stepped forward to meet Dee. This was life, this was opportunity, this was change. She couldn't ask for more.

Venus was the last stand for unaltered humanity, at least for Sienna, and she surrendered willingly.

FLEX AND FLUX

Rosie Oliver

One last sail, one last time to feel a spacecraft's sway and tilt, and not to suffer the crushing constraints of gravity. Even here, two-thirds of the way to the Moon, Ruth enjoyed the challenge of keeping precisely to her course against the whimsical solar wind, the Earth's fluxing magnetosphere and the flexing of Earth's thin atmosphere. She touched her screen to counter a weak ripple from a solar flare, hauling in the left corner of the left spiller sail six centimetres for two seconds.

Ping. She refused to accept the call by waving her hand over the holograph of her Siever spacecraft. It exhibited full sail, with trapezoid and triangular spiller sails either side of a square mainsail. Lines stretched from the sails' eighteen corners to the small blob of her living quarters.

The holograph switched to the head of Lunar Mining, Tsukiko Okumura, in her office overlooking Sinus Iridium. Her hair, as usual, was severely tied back in a knot. Her eyes glanced around, searching the cabin.

Ruth bit her lip. Complaining about the enforced call connect would do her no good.

Tsukiko's eyes lit on Ruth. "Ah, I should have known it was you. I see you're in that old museum piece of a Siever. You must be coming to join us."

"Why should I?"

"Well, in view of your..."

Ruth hated being reminded of the brittle-bone disease which had exiled her from Earth. "I'll never join you. You're nothing better than criminals."

The smile was gone, replaced by a bleak grimness. "We're doing what we must. We need our helium three to synthesise our water. You Earth people are all take, no give."

"Millions will freeze, die even, just because you cut our supplies off without warning."

"We tried to tell your governments. They wouldn't listen. But this argument doesn't extend to you personally. You would always be welcome here if you change your mind. Your alternative is... well, there's no need for me to spell that out."

A shiver went down Ruth's spine. A space station retirement home, more like a crowded rabbit hutch, would be all she could afford. Going to the Moon was worse. She would have to deal with that cold-blooded robot who had forced her out of the only job she could do: helium three-canister handler at the space elevator's high end.

"Go to Hell." She cut the link.

Ruth forced her breathing to slow down, but anger kept her tense and seething. Through a thought maelstrom, one question kept surfacing: *Why did Tsukiko want her to go to the Moon?*

She finally calmed enough to think clearly. *I must be a danger to her. But how?*

Her eyes were drawn to the Siever's holograph. The spacecraft had done the job it was built for: scooping helium three from Earths' Lagrange points. There was none left, nor would there be until the solar wind had replenished the supply several centuries hence. There was nowhere else she could sail this perfectly functioning spacecraft without suffering fatal doses of radiation. She dismissed the thought. Yet Tsukiko's call worried her. *What was she missing?*

She double-checked the space around Earth. Her holographic map showed all the low gravity patches had been swept clean, no surprise there. She examined the asteroid register for Near Earth Objects that could be mined for the fuel. Again, there was no luck. She explored old dust trails left by long gone comets crossing Earth's orbit. There were mere thickenings, but no useful densities of the precious stuff. In desperation she extended her map and all three searches outwards from Earth.

The closest were the Lagrange points along Venus's' orbital path. She did not need to do the calculations to know that sailing there and back would be deadly, and went to wipe the map off. Her hand stopped in mid-air. There would be no harm in doing the calculations, just to have full-blooded proof of the impossibility.

She touch-opted her nav app for round trip trajectories with at least a week's stopover for sieving. Sweeping ponytails filled the holograph's map, all of them various shades of red to warn her they were no-goes. She slumped back in disgust at not trusting her own judgement.

From under the red mass a green line peeked out, going in a crazy direction. It had to be wrong. Singletons like that never happened in spaceflight. She squeezed her eyes shut for a good few seconds. On opening them, the green line was still there, glaring at her.

"Computer, clear all red lines on the trajectory map."
The green line sped from the front Lagrange point, got a gravity assist from Venus and travelled down its tail of Birkeland currents most of the way home. The currents were effectively an extension of the planet's magnetosphere, and would protect her from the harsher solar radiation. No wonder it was a singleton.

She grinned then frowned. This sail looked too easy.

Ruth zoomed in on the Venus flyby to check what margin of error she had. At one point there was only fifteen metres leeway. She whistled. No wonder Tsukiko wanted her out of the way on the Moon. That was tight, more like impossible. But it would be one heck of a sail, where she could feel oh so alive.

She altered her course for Venus's forward orbital Lagrange point.

♀

Ruth flipped the sails to turn her spacecraft back through the densest part of the dust to sieve more He3. Her reactions had already started slowing down, the edge had gone from her thinking and the amount of sleep she needed had crept up. The sooner she had a full load, the sooner she could head for Venus and its protection. Her radiation badge sent out its own message of urgency, with its bar two thirds the way up the safe zone. She stroked it, as if trying to make the damning bar go down.

Ping. Her former boss, Nolan Jaquet in his old office, formed a holograph. A couple of wisps of his hair strayed out of place and dark shadows lingered beneath his eyes. Worse, he had a look of enforced neutrality that was sure to mean trouble.

"Hello Ruth. How are things?"

"Hello Nolan. Get to the point. I'm fine-tuning my sails."

A small smile flickered across his face. "What are you going to do with that He3 you are clearly sieving?"

"What do you think?" She edged one of the sail corners out a tiny bit.

"I know you've been in contact with Tsukiko Okumura."

"Only the once."

"It only takes one conversation to reach an agreement. If there is one in place, we can't negotiate buying your helium three."

"If you think I'll deal with that bitch, think again. What's this 'we' business?"

Nolan took a few seconds to reply. "I'm now employed by our government to find new He3 sources. Boils down to scavenging old gas for remnants, as it's profitable now, just. But that's only a temporary fix. We're building our first unmanned scooper for Uranus's atmosphere, but that'll take years to return. In the meantime, we need to keep looking for contributions to fill the gap."

"So you want my helium three to help you out of a hole?"

"It'll give us a little breathing space, that's all. But yes."

"Aren't you forgetting something?"

"What?"

"I need to get this back to Earth first. With the solar radiation..."

"You've got us puzzled on that one, but I know you too well. You'll have a plan."

"Your scientists and engineers aren't that dumb."

"Not dumb, no. But busy, busy, busy."

"So you haven't worked out what I'm doing? Won't you want others to follow?"

"If it was that easy, you'd have sold your discovery. No, my guess is it involves some danger or requires your specialities."

She nodded. "So how much are you willing to pay for a tank full?"

"The going rate."

"Which is?"

Nolan named a figure.

"That much?"

"I know. It's ridiculous."

Ruth stared at him, unable to believe. She would be rich, in fact rich enough to buy and run a space station condo for life. A twitch of a solar wind isobar on her control screen caught her eye while feeling a tiny bit lighter in her chair. Some very delicate manoeuvring was needed.

"Look, we'll talk later. I need to attend to things here."

"It'll be a pleasure doing business with you."

Nolan flicked out. She let her spiller sail out a little by giving her controls a mere finger-touch and wiggle, a trick she had learned while playing around in her sailing lessons. She felt the slight sway of her craft as it smoothly returned to its original course. At this rate it would only take another couple of days to fill her tank.

♀

Venus blazed cream light through her window. Ruth was forced to narrow her eyes to see, even though her nav screen was set at maximum brightness. A green spider's web spread over it. A blue cross, marking her position, wavered within the innermost circle and orange lines, representing the solar winds, rippled beneath the web. She focussed on keeping the cross in the centre, blindly playing the control screen like an eighteen-note synch-piano, a tap here, a finger drag down there and closing two fingers together in the screen's corner.

A red ellipse shrank slowly inwards. It was the line she must not cross, at any cost, or she would miss catching the tail home. Rivulets and large globules of sweat clung to her face, whether it was from the extra heat or her concentration she wasn't sure.

Ping. Tsukiko was calling her. Ruth hardly noticed and completely ignored it, twisting her mainsail a little upwards.

The cross jerked right.

Her middle finger scrabbled to let out the right trapezoid sail while her thumb glided to let her left spiller sail twist outward to redirect its solar wind back onto the mainsail. The cross edged back towards the web's centre.

The wind's isobars thickened and broke up, forming circles; some sped away while others dwindled into nothing. This violence meant she had reached the boundary where the solar wind dashed against the Venusian magnetosphere, and she would have to sail through it. Her throat went dry, but Ruth kept her concentration up.

She switched the chart to show fifteen kilometres ahead. The wind isobars were denser, whirling in turmoil. This was far worse than expected. It could make her miss her trajectory home.

Panic threatened to make her scream and shake. She forcibly quelled it and zoomed out the wind chart. The sparkling line marking the planet's ozone layer crept onto the screen's right side, but it had a glaring gap of ruin. Isobars bunched up and thrust their way through it from the planet, then crinkled, curled and swirled, before braking up and fading. One hell of a ferocious plume was rising from Venus.

Hands quivering, she radar-checked the surface. Maat Mons was erupting, gushing out lava and gases, and blowing its centuries of pent-up volcanic pressure away. Her course was through the middle of the plume's gusty crest. No way she could keep to it now. All she could do was aim for a series of timed points, reacting as best she could to the wind's buffeting, and hope. It would be one hell of a sail.

Ruth flicked her holograph to the wind map of coloured surfaces, coils and threads. Dominating the mosaic was a ring vortex crowning the plume, which reminded her of the old films of atomic bomb experiments. Shocked, she froze. She knew she had to move, control, fly the Siever. She had to start somewhere. *Look for the stable areas.* The ring was not changing, despite its tornadic winds. Its centre had a still eye. If only it would stay there for the next ten minutes. She prayed she would make it to that transient place of safety.

Her hands stopped trembling and the nerves gnawing at her stomach vanished. An inner peace took over. She concentrated on the wind holograph and its wobbling blue arrow marking her position and direction, while her hands moved blindly, yet with sure instinct, over her sail controls.

Ruth veered round a suddenly formed wind shear, then up and over a curler. The hull whispered of speed under gravity as it hit the solar wind's particles. After weeks of silence, the noise was loud.

The whispering grew louder, becoming a hiss. It flipped from behind her above the centre to right under her. Her spacecraft lurched upwards. Her fingers slipped downwards. She lifted them from the controls, but it was too late. The sails loosened. She felt the tugs on her cabin as they flapped uselessly in the winds. She clawed at the screen's surface. One after another, the five sails resumed their taut curved shapes. Her busy fingers kept them that way through the plume, but she was ready for the next flip.

Silence. She had entered the eye of the storm. Sailing on serenely, she relaxed into her chair and picked out her next aim-point, beyond the edge of the ring vortex where another lull in winds existed.

Moments later, she was back in the noisy plume, struggling to keep her craft steady. Her fingers danced so quickly, they seemed to be doing the impossible of touching all her sail controls at the same time. The noise died. Miraculously, she was on course for Earth. She grinned in triumph.

She eased back, her fingers moving autonomously over the controls navigating the winds' calmer sway and swirl. The cream glow from Venus dimmed until at last it flipped into grey-green ashen light, but it was overwhelmed by the rainbow of lights from her controls. She was in Venus's shadow.

Shading her eyes from the cabin lights with a free hand, she checked the uniform ashen light. A flash of light grey streaked and bloomed across her window, before fading. Then another flash downward, only she thought it crossed a darker line. She blinked. Both lines had vanished.

Everything was calm and for now, the going would be easy.

Ruth had run out of excuses not to check her radiation badge. Hesitantly, she turned her gaze towards it. The red bar was close to the amber line. One little shove would mean nausea and vomiting, the milder symptoms of radiation sickness. She would lose control of her spacecraft. These flight conditions were so unusual that using the autopilot was no good. She'd die, one way or another. Only one tiny nudge... she shivered as if someone had walked over her grave.

Gritting her teeth, she flicked the holograph to the electromagnetic map of the tail. A long translucent red cone of protons extended from behind Venus, its point almost reaching Earth's orbital path. Inside, a dark blue double helix of Birkeland currents rising from the planet shone so steady she could sail along its almost neutral radiation path blindfolded. Light blue loops surrounding the helixes' bases grew and shrank back down, minor Birkeland currents brought about by the local weather conditions.

The cone, double helix and loops wobbled.

Ruth yelped and clutched her armrests. She tried to get rid of the memory. It wouldn't go away.

It shook again. The push briefly thrust the cone away from Maat Mons. She gasped as understanding dawned. The eruption was sending magnetic waves around the planet. Her sailing skills were no match for the spontaneity and extent of the movement.

She was a dead woman sailing. Her mind fogged with paralysis. She had to find some protection from the deadly gamma radiation in open space. Only her sails stopped that, but they were her ticket home.

Correction, her mainsail, trapezoid sails and one spiller sail for control were all she really needed. The steering would be far more difficult, nevertheless perhaps possible. That left the issue of wrapping a spiller sail round her cabin. Now that was impossible. Nobody had done that; even the most inept sailors doing idiot things had not done that. *It's different here. The solar wind is denser and gives me more manoeuvring power.*

An idea formed. She prodded and poked at it to rubbish

it, only to end up refining it. It could work. She had nothing more to lose, and the rest of her life to gain.

Her fingers sprang to life, flicking so fast over the controls they became blurred. She reeled out two lines on the left spiller sail, while keeping the outermost corner firmly in position, and steering her spacecraft into the double helix's Birkeland current streaming away from Venus. A glance at the radiation level showed it was tolerable. She reeled out the final corner of the left spiller, far enough to comfortably loop it under her cabin to the other side.

She paused, flexing her fingers. Taking a deep breath, she gently lowered her fingertips onto the screen and looked out of her left window. The spiller sail, dimly illuminated by her navigation lights, was spread out flat just as it should be. Ruth yanked in all the upper corners of her other sails. She watched the spiller sail drop down out of sight, then pulled in right corners of all the other sails in succession from the right spiller through the left trapezoid. Her holograph showed her cabin start to swing over the left spiller.

The nervous sweat of being too eager to hit the controls drenched her. She bit her lip, determined to hold back until the right moment, but fearing she might react too late. Her hands jittered over the control screen, to touch, or to not touch.

Ruth hit the screen hard, with all her fingers.

Four sails unfurled to catch as much wind as possible. Her spacecraft tugged forward. Her left spiller drifted behind her. She prayed the left spiller lines would have enough momentum to continue going right. Seconds grew into eternities. The left spiller lines slowed. She waited, watched the holograph and waited, pools of sweat forming on her face.

The line to the outermost point of the spiller finally cleared the other side of cabin. She pulled the sail in, a touch on that corner, a pat on this and a slow draw-in on the other. Her eyes were aching from focusing for too long. She shook her head to give them some relief. Beads of sweat sprayed off her face. She snatched at swiping them away; too busy delicately manipulating the spiller, while trying to stay on course. The spacecraft was slipping out of her control. She became frantic, her fingers frenetic.

The spiller thudded the rear of her cabin, jerking her fingers forward onto the control screen. "No..."

She scraped back as much of her error as she could. A line cracked against the hull's side as it tightened too quickly. Checking confirmed the hull was still intact. A corner of the sail slapped onto the hull's bottom. She pulled at the other lines. Rasping echoed throughout her cabin as the sail slid over the whole of the hull. Ruth tightened the lines.

She was safe. The sail cocooned her cabin except for the front that faced homeward, away from the Sun's glare and radiation. She relaxed.

A throbbing pain in her hands hit her. She cursed, trying to move them into a more comfortable position. Nothing worked. In the end she took painkillers so she could continue navigating her spacecraft down the spiralling Birkeland current towards home.

The red bar on her radiation badge remained under the amber line even now, two days after leaving Venus. Ruth smiled, luxuriating in sipping the full-bodied Tregothnan tea from her specialised tea-making bulb, a treat she had kept back for a moment like this. She would make it home, and see the blue oceans, the glowing white polar caps, the vibrant green of the forests, the mottled browns and yellows of deserts and mountains, and the wafting streaks and fluffs of clouds.

Ping.

The menace of Tsukiko and her grasping ways could not shift her mood. She waved a refusal to accept.

The orange starlight of old faithful Aldebaran peered in through the window, still sitting at the spiller's top edge. It was good to have something constant in her life.

She choked on her tea. The spiller sail should have long since blocked her view of Aldebaran. Handing her drink bulb back to its holder, she pulled up her control console onto her screen. The diagram of her actual trajectory had veered away from her planned course the moment she had wrapped the sail around her cabin.

"What in the seven hells?" Another two hours would have seen her drift out the Birkeland current altogether.

Peering out of the window, her fingers went to work to manoeuvre the Siever back on course. She pulled the right hand corners of her main and trapezoid sails in. She angled the right spiller sail to push more onto the left trapezoid sail. Far too slowly, Aldebaran drifted towards and then behind the sail. She let her spacecraft continue veer round until the Hyades star group was next to her sail, exactly where it should have been.

Ruth bit her lip, trying to figure out why she had veered off course by so much. She did the usual functionality checks on her console. Perfect working order. The lines' checks came back showing nothing wrong there. The agent checks showed all sails as being fully intact. That left only the navigation sensors, some having been blocked by the enshrouding spiller sail. *Garbage in, garbage out.* The old computer saying, drummed into her at school, was very relevant here. Her flight management system could not deal with so many sensors out of action.

"Damn and double damn!"

The errors would have to be compensated for manually. She stared down at her hands. They were steady, not even the slightest twitch, so different from when she had flown past Venus. She had the confidence to do it, and had had it ever since flying through the plume. She would navigate home over the coming weeks by hand and star-by-star.

Ruth sat back and taking hold of her drink bulb, took a sip of her precious tea. She was going to enjoy the challenge.

♀

Her muscles ached from overuse, her eyes itched from forcing herself to stay awake and her seat felt overly uncomfortable from sitting too long in it. She no longer needed the stars to guide her, instead she was using Earth's geography to precision direct her sails. Another two days and she would be safely inside Earth's magnetosphere.

Ping.

Ruth ignored it.

Ping again.

"Go away," she muttered as she eased her finger down the screen.

Ping a third time.

She glanced at the missed call list. Two were from Tsukiko. The third was Nolan. She waved acceptance of the last.

Nolan's smiling rapidly turned to horror. "Damn it, Ruth, you look awful."

"Is that any way to greet an old friend?"

"It is when I see you like this. What's up?"

"Lack of sleep."

Nolan narrowed his eyes. "Are you sure?"

"Yes. What else can it be?"

"Radiation? According to our calcs—"

"I should be on my deathbed. Yes, I know." She held up her radiation badge with its red bar still below the amber line. "Sorry to disappoint."

His mouth dropped. "How, in God's name?"

"You wouldn't believe me if I told you the truth."

"Like that, is it?"

"Yep."

"I'm sending out a hauler to tow you back in."

"Like hell you are. I know the laws of salvage as well as you do."

"So does Tsukiko. She's got a hauler ready to roll down her catapult."

"She can get lost."

"She's going to try. I feel it in my bones."

Ruth blinked in surprise. "Sounds like Tsukiko's burning all her bridges with Earth."

"Well and truly."

"Ouch." Ruth had never liked dealing with politics, but she would deal with it in her own way now. "I'd be happy for you to escort me in. That should keep her away."

"I'm on my way."

"Let me make one thing very clear, I'm sailing to the space elevator on the winds and a prayer."

"Ruth—"

"No arguments."

"You were never like this. What happened to you out there?"

Ruth smiled. "Let's just say I learned not to accept, but to do."

ABOUT THE AUTHORS

Heidi Kneale

Heidi Kneale is an Australian author of moderate repute best known for her escapist fiction. She lives in Western Australia, near the ocean. Like most humans, she's got a family. She also associates with the World's Most Boring Cat. When not writing novels, she composes music and stares at the stars.

Deborah Walker

Deborah Walker grew up in the most English town in the country, but she soon high-tailed it down to London, where she now lives with her partner, Chris, and her two young children. Find Deborah in the British Museum trawling the past for future inspiration. Her stories have appeared in *Fantastic Stories of the Imagination*, *Nature Futures*, *Lady Churchill's Rosebud Wristlet* and *The Year's Best SF 18* and have been translated into over a dozen languages.

EM Edwards

EM Edwards was born in San Francisco but grew up in an ex-mining town, amid mercury tainted ponds and cyanide sands. A place which still annually bleeds riches and poisons in abundance from its rust-red soil. He studied biological sciences at the University of California at Davis before moving to Berkeley. There he worked on artificial intelligence and spent his dreaming hours in the unlit trenches of the Monterey Submarine Canyon. He now lives on the South East coast of England where he writes fiction.

Lorraine Schein

Lorraine Schein is a New York writer who used to be a part-time anarchist. Her work has appeared in *Gargoyle, New*

Letters, Hotel Amerika, Nonbinary Review, Mad Scientist Journal, Evil Girlfriend Media, and the anthologies *Gigantic Worlds, Drawn to Marvel,* and *My Favorite Apocalypse.* Her poetry book, *The Futurist's Mistress,* is available from mayapplepress.com. She used to work at Marvel Comics and is now working on a graphic novel.

Erin M Hartshorn

Erin M Hartshorn lives in Pennsylvania with her husband, two children, and English cocker spaniel. A member of SFWA and the Garden State Speculative Fiction Writers, Erin has had fiction published at *Clarkesworld Magazine* and *Daily Science Fiction* as well as in various anthologies. She also publishes mysteries under the pen name Sara Penhallow; her most recent release is *The Corn Maze Murders.* She blogs online at www.erinmhartshorn.com/blog and can be found on Twitter @ErinMHartshorn.

Rosie Oliver

Rosie is a systems engineer of over thirty years standing, but took time out for an MA in Creative Writing at Bath Spa University. She enjoys writing progressive science fiction, which shows how people and computers embrace and develop with their changing environments. Her short stories have been published in various magazines and anthologies. After having had a series of standalone stories published about a self-learner robo-cat, called C.A.T., she is currently writing his novel.

ALSO AVAILABLE FROM
WHIPPLESHIELD BOOKS

Adrift on the Sea of Rains

Ian Sales

Winner of the BSFA Award
Finalist for the Sidewise Award

"scrupulously researched, written with an expert blend of technical precision, descriptive vividness and emotional penetration; it's a Cold War alt-historical gem"
Adam Roberts, author of *The Thing Itself*

- paperback   £4.99 / $7.50 / €6.00
- ebook: PDF, EPUB, MOBI   £2.99 / $3.99 / €2.99

The Eye With Which The Universe Beholds Itself

Ian Sales

"...combines solidly-researched Space Age hardware and truthful human psychology with bold but plausible speculative physics, in a slingshot trajectory to an alt-space, alt-history future that boldly goes"
Ken MacLeod, author of *Descent*

- paperback	£4.99 / $7.50 / €6.00
- signed numbered hardback	£6.99 / $12.00 / €8.50
- ebook: PDF, EPUB, MOBI	£2.99 / $3.99 / €2.99

Then Will The Great Ocean Wash Deep Above

Ian Sales

"An impressive depth of research combined with a love of space programs is aptly married to excellent writing."

SF Signal

- paperback   £4.99 / $6.50 / €6.00
- signed numbered hardback   £6.99 / $10.00 / €8.50
- ebook: PDF, EPUB, MOBI   £2.99 / $3.99 / €2.99

All That Outer Space Allows

Ian Sales

"absorbing and undeniably powerful, and takes risks that I wish I encountered more frequently in the genre"
Nerds of a Feather

- paperback   £7.99 / $9.50 / €9.00
- signed numbered hardback   £9.99 / $13.00 / €11.50
- ebook: PDF, EPUB, MOBI   £2.99 / $3.99 / €2.99

Dreams of the Space Age

Ian Sales

A collection of seven tales of alternate Space Ages, from the first man in space to the first man to leave the Solar System, from the wives of the astronauts to the husband and wife team who first set foot on Mars. With an introduction by Dave Hutchinson, author of *Europe in Autumn* and *Europe at Midnight*.

- paperback	£4.99 / $7.50 / €6.00
- signed numbered hardback	£6.99 / $10.00 / €8.50
- ebook: PDF, EPUB, MOBI	£1.99 / $2.99 / €2.99